GW00994160

THE TÁIN

The Great Celtic Epic

THE TÁIN

The Great Celtic Epic

LIAM Mac UISTIN

Illustrations by
DONALD TESKEY

THE O'BRIEN PRESS
DUBLIN

First published 1989 by The O'Brien Press Ltd.
Copyright © text Liam Mac Uistin;
Copyright © illustrations The O'Brien Press.

All rights reserved. No part of this book may be reproduced
or utilised in any way or by any means, electronic or mechanical,
including photocopying, recording or by any information storage and retrieval
system without permission in writing from the publisher. This book may not
be sold as a remainder, bargain book or at a reduced price without
permission in writing from the publisher.

British Library Cataloguing in Publication Data
Mac Uistin, Liam
The Tain: The great celtic epic
1. Irish tales and legends
I. Title
398.2'09415
ISBN 0-86278-204-X

Typeset at The O'Brien Press
Book design: Michael O'Brien
Printed by Billings & Sons Ltd, Worcester

The O'Brien Press receives assistance
from The Arts Council/
An Chomhairle Ealaíon, Ireland.

For Brian, with love.

The Background and Setting of the Táin

THE TÁIN IS ONE OF THE MOST ANCIENT IRISH STORIES. Scholars say it was passed from generation to generation by word of mouth. It tells of an ancient Celtic culture, a culture of war, cattle raids, warriors, beheadings, chariot-fighting, honour and bravery.

The earliest written versions do not give the complete story in any single manuscript, but sections are contained in the early twelfth-century *Book of the Dun Cow* and in the fourteenth-century *Yellow Book of Lecan*.

The *Táin* does more than simply tell a good story. It tells us how those people of long-forgotten days lived and what they thought was good and bad, right and wrong. As the story shows, they believed that disaster can result from overpowering greed and jealousy; honour is important, and keeping one's word is one of the higher values; cunning and trickery can be used for both good and evil. In the *Táin* all human emotions are writ large - jealousy, brotherly love, justice, treachery, humour, duty - everything is here in its most powerful form.

The *Táin* story also tells us that these people believed that humans were not alone in the world. Other worlds exist and other beings - fairies, the Tuatha de Danaan - enter into the human world from time to time, bringing both good and evil and frequently providing magical powers and skills to get people out of tight situations. Thus Cuchulainn has his Ga Bolga, the weapon nobody can withstand, and he gets special superhuman powers when he goes into battle, making him the equal of hundreds if not thousands. The warrior-queen Maeve can call on her druid to weave a magic spell, putting the Ulster army to sleep - however, the spell has no effect on Cuchulainn who represents good in the story. She also calls on the evil Morrigan to trick him, but again he finally triumphs over her powers, although he is badly injured in the combat. Good and evil tussle right through the story, and people are constantly helped or put in danger by these magical powers.

This is a story from a warrior culture, where defending one's territory is of prime importance. In this culture cattle are the chief form of wealth (taking the place of money in today's world) and cattle raids seem to have been frequent means of adding to one's wealth. This is not a peaceful society. Its greatest heroes are its greatest warriors, both men and women. Women like Maeve and Emer play a very important role in it.

But efforts are made to keep peace. Fostering is used as a means of developing feelings of kinship and in the story we see foster brothers Cuchulainn and Ferdia reluctantly face each other at the borders of Ulster. Ferdia has been tricked into fighting to defend his honour and he cannot go back on his word, but neither wants to fight the other. We see how close foster brothers can be and we share in the sadness of the awful situation they face.

War, peace, love, greed, fate, these are the stuff of an epic, and in the *Táin* they are present in full.

Ide ní Laoghaire

CHAPTER ONE

How the Táin Began

QUEEN MAEVE WAS VERY ANGRY. Her eyes flashed with fury as she strode into the hall of her palace at Cruachan. Her anger swelled when she heard the mocking laughter of her husband Ailill drifting in from the garden. A fierce look of determination came over her face. She, the mighty Warrior Queen of Connacht, would not be mocked by anyone!

'I will make Ailill regret his challenge!' she vowed. She clapped her hands and shouted for her servants.

The trouble all began just a short while before when Maeve and Ailill set out on their usual morning walk in the garden. The previous night they had quarrelled over which of them was the wealthier. But when they woke the next morning the quarrel seemed to be forgotten and they went for their stroll together arm-in-arm.

It was a lovely summer morning and the air was full of the sweet singing of birds and the drowsy murmuring of bees. Maeve smiled contentedly and combed away a strand of hair that the playful breeze had tossed into her beautiful face.

But though Maeve was very beautiful she was also very proud. From the time she was a little girl she had been used to getting her own way. Her father, the High King of Ireland, adored her and gave her anything she wanted.

When she reached her twenty-first year he asked her what present she would like.

'I want a whole province of Ireland to rule over as queen,' she said.

'Very well,' her father said. 'I will give you the province of Connacht.'

Maeve built a magnificent palace of white gleaming stone at Cruachan. She filled the palace with her many treasures and possessions and put her great herds of animals on the lands around it. She had hundreds of servants to look after her and thousands of soldiers to guard her. If any chieftain displeased her she would jump into her war chariot and lead out her soldiers to teach him a lesson. She was soon known far and wide as 'The Warrior Queen of Connacht.'

Princes came from all over Ireland hoping to marry the rich and beautiful queen. But none of them attracted her and she sent them all away. Then Ailill, son of the king of Leinster, came to visit her at Cruachan. Perhaps it was his good looks or his haughty bearing – whatever the reason, she fell in love with him immediately. They married a short while later and Ailill brought all his treasures and herds to Cruachan.

But Ailill was every bit as proud of his riches as Maeve was of hers. And this was the cause of the row between them as they walked in the garden that lovely morning.

Noticing the serene way she looked he remarked, 'You seem very happy today, my dear.'

'I am very happy indeed,' she assured him with a warm smile.

'And you have every reason to be,' Ailill said. 'You are, after all, the wife of the richest person in Ireland.'

A frown of annoyance clouded Maeve's face. 'What do you mean?' she demanded. 'Everyone knows I'm far wealthier than you.'

'Nonsense!' Ailill retorted. 'Nobody in the whole land has more treasures and herds than I.' They stopped and stood there arguing heatedly about their riches.

'Enough!' Ailill declared finally. 'There's only one way to settle this matter. I challenge you to have everything we own brought here and counted and compared to see who has the most.'

'I accept your challenge!' Maeve snapped. 'And you will be sorry you ever made it.' She turned on her heel and marched back to the palace.

'There's no fear of that,' Ailill called after her and he burst out laughing at the very idea.

Back in the palace Maeve stamped her foot angrily and shouted again for her servants. They came running from every direction, trembling with fright when they saw the furious expression on her face. She ordered them to collect all her possessions and those of her husband and bring them out to the garden. Then she returned to where Ailill was still laughing. 'Now I shall prove that I am wealthier than you,' she said triumphantly.

First, their gleaming goblets and valuable vases were brought out, together with all their precious jewels and shining ornaments of silver and gold. But when they were counted and compared they were found to be equal in value and number.

Next, their great herds of horses and sheep were brought from the fields and counted. Maeve's herds matched those of Ailill in size and number.

Then all their cattle were collected and brought before them. When they were counted and compared they were found to be equal in number and size except for one animal in Ailill's herd. This was a magnificent-looking bull called Finnbeannach.

'I told you,' Ailill gloated. 'I am wealthier than you.'

Maeve did not reply. She was almost crying with anger. She could not believe that she owned no animal to equal Finnbeannach. She stormed back into the palace and shouted for Mac Roth, her Chief Messenger.

Mac Roth rushed into the hall and stood before her, leaning on his staff as he tried to catch his breath.

'Do you know of any place in Ireland where a bull the equal of Finnbeannach can be found?' Maeve asked.

'Yes, I do,' Mac Roth replied. 'There's a much finer bull in Cooley in Ulster. It's known as the Brown Bull of Cooley.'

'Who owns it?'

'A man named Daire Mac Fiachna.'

'Will he sell it to me?'

'I doubt it.'

'Will he lend it then?'

'He might be prepared to oblige the great Queen of Connacht.'

'Go to him immediately,' Maeve commanded. 'Ask him to lend me the bull for one year. Tell him I'll pay him handsomely. I'll give him fifty of my finest heifers and the Brown Bull back at the end of the year.'

The Chief Messenger hesitated and shook his head doubtfully.

'Conor, King of Ulster, may not allow it and the people of Ulster may not let Daire part with the bull either,' he said. 'It's a jewel of an animal and they're very proud of it. There could be trouble if they saw me taking it away.'

Maeve waved her hand dismissively. 'Tell Daire in that event to bring it here himself,' she said. 'As well as the heifers, I'll give him as much land as he wants and a splendid chariot and my own undying friendship to crown it all.'

So Mac Roth set out for Cooley accompanied by nine other messengers. But he grew more worried with every mile that passed. He wondered anxiously how Daire would receive him. He was pleasantly surprised when he arrived at Daire's house and was given a warm welcome. Daire was a fat jolly little man who felt flattered by a visit from Maeve's Chief Messenger. He put Mac Roth sitting on a nice soft cushion and began to chat about this and that. After a while Mac Roth turned the conversation around to the purpose of his visit.

He explained about the rivalry between Maeve and her husband and how the queen wanted a loan of the Brown Bull to match it against Finnbeannach. Then he went on to describe the generous payment that Maeve was prepared to offer.

A broad smile spread over Daire's face when he heard that. He bounced up and down with joy and suddenly burst the cushion he was sitting on!

'Of course I'll lend the Brown Bull to the queen!' he declared.

Mac Roth was very relieved. The mission has been successful, he thought. Maeve will be very pleased. But later that night something happened that upset all their plans.

Daire had arranged for the messengers from Connacht to be given comfortable quarters and the best of food and drink. During the feast the messengers grew drunk and noisy. One of them stood up and banged on the table with his goblet.

'Let us drink a toast to Daire,' he proposed. 'It was good of him to give us the Brown Bull so willingly.'

Another man stood up and laughed scornfully. 'If it hadn't been given willingly we'd have taken it by force!' he declared.

Shouts of agreement rang out around the table. One of Daire's servants was infuriated by this and ran out to his master.

'Did you promise to give our treasure the Brown Bull to those messengers from Connacht?' he asked.

'I did,' replied Daire.

'What they said then must be true.'

'What did they say?'

'They boasted that if you hadn't given it willingly they would have taken it by force.'

Daire's eyes blazed suddenly with anger. 'I swear by the gods that the Brown Bull will never leave Ulster now!' he vowed, clutching the dagger in his belt.

Unaware of what had happened Mac Roth came to see Daire the next morning. 'Tell me where the bull is so we can take him away,' he said.

'I will not!' snapped Daire. 'And only that I'm not in the habit of killing messengers none of you would leave this place alive.'

Mac Roth stared at him in astonishment. 'Why do you say that?' he asked.

'Because your men swore they'd take the bull by force if I didn't give it willingly.'

Mac Roth shook his head. 'Don't mind their silly talk. They must have taken too much drink.'

'Even so. I'll never part with the Brown Bull as long as I can help it.'

'I apologise for … ' Mac Roth started to say, but Daire cut him short with an angry gesture.

'You and your men must leave my house at once!' he ordered.

His face bitter with disappointment, Mac Roth summoned the other messengers and led them back empty-handed to Cruachan. Immediately she heard of their return Maeve ran out eagerly to meet them.

'Where is the Brown Bull of Cooley?' she asked.

With a woeful expression, Mac Roth explained what had happened. The queen was furious.

'I will own that animal,' she said in a harsh voice. 'Even if I have to take it from Ulster by force.'

'But that means a *Táin*, a great cattle-raid …' Mac Roth protested.

'Yes, and I shall lead it!' Maeve snapped. 'Tell my warriors to prepare at once for war!'

And so the *Táin* began.

CHAPTER TWO

Preparing for War

MAEVE SAT IN A QUIET CORNER of the garden and thought long and carefully about the coming clash with the men of Ulster. Her rage now had died away. It had been replaced by a feeling of ice-cold determination. She knew it would be no easy task to defeat King Conor and his warriors. The King of Ulster and his men would fiercely resist any invasion of their province.

But defeat them she must! Her own honour was at stake as well as the great prize of the Brown Bull of Cooley. She thought for another while about what she would do. Then her face broke into a smile. She would get her allies to help her! She had many friends in Munster and Leinster and some of them were among the bravest warriors in Ireland. With them at her side she would be sure of victory!

She jumped to her feet and strode back to the palace. She summoned Mac Roth and ordered him to go to all her allies and tell them she needed their help. The Chief Messenger set off immediately in his chariot.

Maeve's warrior friends poured into Cruachan from all directions. The queen's eyes shone with delight when she saw the vast army that had gathered around her. It included many who bore a grudge against King Conor and were only too happy to settle old scores with him. Among them was a group of Ulstermen led by Fergus Mac Roich from whom Conor had taken the kingship of Ulster by force.

But a little niggling doubt still worried Queen Maeve. She wanted to be absolutely sure of success. So she sent for her Chief Druid to see what the future held in store. The druid was an old wrinkled man famous for his prophecies.

'Tell me,' Maeve said, 'will I return victorious from the *Táin*?'

The druid raised his snake-shaped wand and gazed at it.

'You will return safely,' he prophesied.

'But will I defeat the army of Ulster?'

The druid hesitated, then raised his wand again.

'I see no sign of it here,' he said.

'I must defeat them!' Maeve hissed, stamping her foot impatiently.

'You'll need some magic to help you if you wish to be sure of that,' the druid declared. 'I'll put a spell on Conor and his men so that they'll fall into an enchanted sleep.'

He waved his wand and began to cast a spell.

Just at that moment King Conor and his warriors were enjoying a great feast in his palace at Eman Macha. Some were drinking, some were eating, some were listening to the music of

the harp when suddenly they fell into a deep sleep.

Only one warrior there was not affected by the spell. His name was Cuchulainn.

'The Ulstermen are asleep,' the druid announced to Maeve. The queen laughed triumphantly. 'Nothing can stop me now!' she said. 'The Brown Bull will soon be mine!'

She ran to her war chariot, leaped into it, and waved to her army to follow her. And so they set off for Ulster.

But Fergus Mac Roich was unhappy as he followed the queen. Cuchulainn was his foster-son and he felt he should warn him of Maeve's trickery. He called one of his men and ordered him to take a message to Cuchulainn.

When the messenger arrived at Eman Macha there was a strange silence in the palace. He went into the feasting hall. Cuchulainn was running around from one table to another trying frantically to wake up the sleeping men. He glanced up warily as the messenger entered the hall.

'You are wasting your time,' the messenger said. 'Those men are in an enchanted sleep.'

'Who are you?' Cuchulainn asked.

'I've been sent by Fergus to warn you,' the messenger replied. And he explained what Maeve had done. 'She now thinks that Ulster is defenceless,' he concluded.

'Well it's not,' Cuchulainn said grimly. 'I'll put a stop to this invasion.'

He hurried from the palace and raced to where his charioteer Laeg was waiting for him.

'Yoke up the horses,' he ordered. When the chariot was ready

he jumped in beside Laeg, took the reins, and drove like a whirlwind to a river ford some miles away. He knew that Maeve and her army would have to cross here on their way into Ulster.

He leaped from the chariot before it came to a halt. Then, drawing his sword he hacked a large fork from a tree and wedged it firmly in the middle of the ford.

'Now,' he said. 'No chariot will have room to pass here.'

But just at that moment four of Maeve's advance guard arrived at the ford. They paused for an instant and then with bloodthirsty whoops launched themselves at him. Cuchulainn sliced each of their spears in two. Then he killed them and cut off their heads. He placed the heads on the tree fork and crossed back over the river.

'Let us make camp before nightfall,' he said to Laeg. The charioteer whipped up the horses and they drove away to a nearby wood.

Soon afterwards Maeve and her army reached the ford. The queen stared in amazement at the heads stuck on the tree fork. 'Do those belong to warriors of mine?' she asked.

'Yes,' replied Fergus, 'and very good warriors too.'

'Who did this?'

'A man called Cuchulainn. He is also known as the Hound of Ulster.'

'He must have escaped the druid's spell. Is he a giant?'

'No, he is a small beardless youth.'

'Well, whatever he is he's still only one man,' Maeve snorted contemptuously.

'Yes, but he's not like any other man,' Fergus said. 'He can do most marvellous deeds.' He paused and added, 'He always could, even when he was very young.'

And he began to tell her the story of Cuchulainn.

CHAPTER THREE

The Story of Cuchulainn

CUCHULAINN WAS THE ONLY SON OF SUALDAM, an Ulster nobleman. His mother was Deichtire, sister of King Conor. When he was born he was given the name Setanta. His godfather was the great Lug of the Long Arm, famed for his magical powers. He gave some of these powers as a gift to his godson.

Setanta lived with his parents in a very lonely part of Ulster. He had no playmates so he had to amuse himself. His favourite toys were his hurley-stick and spear and he spent long hours playing with them every day. But though he became very skilful at these games he often pined for the company of other boys.

Then one day he heard his parents talking about a special school at Eman Macha for the sons of noblemen. King Conor himself supervised their training in hurling and athletics. Setanta was interested immediately. This was the place for him!

But when he asked his mother to send him there she shook her head firmly.

'No, you're far too young,' she said.

'Please,' he begged. 'I'd love to go. And besides, I've never met my uncle the king.'

'All in good time,' his mother smiled. 'You can go to school and meet my brother in another few years.'

'But I don't want to wait,' Setanta said.

'Well, you'll have to. Your father and I are too busy to take you there now.'

'Tell me how to get to Eman Macha and I'll go there myself.'

'The road is northwards over Slieve Fuaid. It's too long and difficult for a little boy like you.'

But Setanta continued to plead with his mother and she finally agreed to let him go. His heart thumped with excitement as he set off with his toy spear, shield, hurley-stick and silver ball.

To shorten the journey he played his favourite game. He hurled the ball a long distance ahead of him. Then he flung his hurley-stick after it, striking it in mid-air so that it travelled another long distance ahead. While the stick and ball were still in the air he threw his spear after them and raced like a deer to catch all three before they hit the ground.

He amused himself this way until he arrived at Eman Macha. The boys from the school were playing a game of hurling. Setanta watched for a while and then ran out on the field to join them.

The other boys were not too pleased to see him. No stranger was allowed in their games unless he had first sought their protection. But Setanta was not aware of this rule.

He burst into a group of boys and took possession of the ball. Then he steered the ball with his hurley to the end of the field, running so fast that no one could stop him.

He turned around smiling, only to see a crowd of furious boys advancing on him from all sides. They suddenly closed in on him and flung their hurley-sticks at him. But Setanta skipped this way and that, avoiding all the sticks. Then they threw their spears at him but he blocked them all with his toy shield. By now he too was furious at the rough reception he was getting. He charged at the boys, knocking most of them to the ground and scattering the rest around the field.

Some of the boys ran for their lives towards the palace. Setanta raced after them, angrily brandishing his spear. King Conor was

sitting in his garden playing a game of chess. He looked up in astonishment when the fleeing boys suddenly burst into the garden and leaped over the chess-board, with Setanta hot on their heels. Conor reached out and caught him in a firm grip.

'Let me go!' Setanta yelped, struggling to free himself.

'Easy on now,' Conor said. 'Why are you treating those boys so roughly?'

'Because that's the way they treated me when I joined in their game. The king won't be pleased when I tell him about this.'

'I am the king. And who might you be?'

'I am your nephew, Setanta.'

Conor smiled and released his grip. 'Well, I'm delighted to meet you,' he said, 'even if you have upset my pupils.'

'It's their own fault,' Setanta said. 'They shouldn't have turned on me when I tried to play with them.'

'Don't you know you should have looked for their protection first?'

'No.'

'We must stick to the rules,' the king said quietly. He called the boys together and ordered them to give the newcomer their protection. Then he told them to return to the field and start the game again. He went to watch them as they played.

Setanta got possession of the ball and raced away with it, knocking boys down like nine-pins. Conor called him over.

'You'll injure my pupils if you're not careful,' he said.

'Perhaps they'd better look for my protection,' Setanta suggested.

The king nodded. 'I think that would be best,' he agreed.

So Setanta promised protection to the other boys and they resumed their game. Conor was very pleased with the way his nephew outshone the others in skill and courage. He was convinced the boy would grow up to be a great warrior.

'And so he did,' Fergus said to Maeve, finishing his tale of Setanta.

'But how did he get the name "Cuchulainn"?' the queen asked.

'That's another story,' Fergus replied. 'And I'll tell it to you now.

CHAPTER FOUR

How Cuchulainn Got His Name

SETANTA QUICKLY SETTLED INTO THE SCHOOL at Eman Macha. Soon he became its star pupil. No other boy could beat him at running, at wrestling, at hurling, or at spear-throwing. Conor was very proud of him. He boasted about his nephew's feats to all his friends and introduced him to every distinguished visitor to the palace.

One day the king received an invitation to a feast at the house of Culann his blacksmith. As Culann had never met Setanta, the king decided to bring the boy along with him. He went to the field where Setanta was playing a hurling match.

'I'm going to a feast at Culann's house,' he called out. 'I'd like you to come with me.'

'Let me finish this game first,' pleaded Setanta.

'Very well,' Conor replied. 'You can follow on after me as soon as it's finished.'

Then he set off for the feast accompanied by his bodyguards. He received a royal welcome from Culann who led him to the place of honour at the table.

'Is there anybody still to come after you?' Culann asked the king.

'No,' Conor answered, forgetting all about Setanta.

'I keep a savage hound to guard my house,' Culann explained. 'I'll set him loose outside before the feast begins.'

He took the hound off the chain and put him outside. Then he locked the door and returned to his guests. The huge hound sat in front of the house snapping his sharp teeth and growling fiercely.

When Setanta finished the game he hurried off to follow his uncle. He took his hurley-stick, ball, and spear with him, throwing them ahead of him as he went on the journey. So interested was he in this game that he failed to notice the hound when he arrived at Culann's house.

A sudden savage growl warned him of danger. He turned quickly and saw the hound just as it sprang at him with gnashing teeth. His hurley and spear were still twirling high in the air so he had no weapon to defend himself. But luckily the ball was in his hand.

The snapping jaws were reaching for his face when Setanta flung the ball with all his might down the hound's throat. The animal stopped, choked, and collapsed on the ground. It lay there, growling angrily with its dying breath.

The men inside the house heard the commotion. A sudden silence fell on the feast. Conor jumped up with a look of horror on his face. 'My nephew!' he gasped. 'I forgot that I told him to follow me here.'

Culann rose ashen-faced from the table. 'I fear my hound may have killed him,' he said in a trembling voice. He called his servants. 'Go out at once and see what's happened to the boy.'

The servants rushed out. They stared in amazement as Setanta stood there with his foot on the dead hound. Then they brought him into the house.

'You're alive!' Conor exclaimed joyfully.

'Yes, but I'm afraid the hound is dead,' Setanta said.

Culann could not conceal his anger. 'You are welcome here for your uncle's sake but not for your own sake,' he said icily. 'You have deprived me of the best watchdog in the land.'

'Don't be angry,' Setanta said. 'I'll find another hound for you.'

'And what will I do in the meantime?' Culann asked

'I shall be your faithful watchdog,' Setanta replied.

'From now on you will be called Cuchulainn, "The Hound of Culann"!' the king declared.

'And that has been his name ever since,' Fergus said to Maeve as he concluded the tale.

The queen stared thoughtfully at the heads of her warriors stuck on the tree fork in the middle of the ford. This Cuchulainn could prove to be a formidable enemy. She had better learn all there was to be known about him.

'Tell me some more about this extraordinary man,' she said to Fergus.

CHAPTER FIVE

Cuchulainn and Emer

CUCHULAINN GREW VERY RESTLESS after four years at the school in Eman Macha. Though still only a boy he was impatient to become a warrior. He decided to ask King Conor for permission to take the arms of manhood.

The king shook his head. 'It is too soon for that,' he said. 'You must wait some more years.'

'But I have already learned all the skills of combat,' Cuchulainn argued.

'There are other things you have yet to learn,' Conor declared. 'My Chief Druid has come to instruct the pupils in druid lore. Go now and hear what he has to say.'

Cuchulainn went off reluctantly to join the other boys. He sat there with a bored expression on his face as the tall silver-haired druid rose to begin his talk. But soon he was listening with fascination to the tales of magic and mystery.

At the end of the talk a pupil stood up and asked what that day would be favourable for.

'Whoever assumes arms for the first time today will become the most famous warrior in Ireland,' the druid said. He paused and added, 'But his life will be short and fleeting.'

Immediately he heard this, Cuchulainn rushed out and went back to King Conor. He pleaded again to be allowed take arms. The king was silent for a while. Then impressed by the eagerness in his nephew's eyes he smiled and nodded.

'I cannot refuse you,' he said. He handed Cuchulainn a sword, spear, and shield. 'Now you are a warrior.'

Cuchulainn shook the weapons to test them. They fell to pieces in his hands. 'These arms are useless!' he exclaimed in disgust.

The king sighed. 'I'll give you my own arms,' he said. 'They're the only ones you'll never break.'

As he was presenting the weapons to Cuchulainn the Chief Druid entered the room. 'Is your nephew taking arms?' he asked.

'He is,' Conor replied.

'Well, he who does so for the first time today will be great and famous,' the druid said. 'But his life will be a short one.'

There was silence for a moment. Then Cuchulainn shrugged and smiled. 'I don't care if I live for only a day and a night,' he declared, 'provided my fame lives after me.'

And so Cuchulainn became a warrior. By the time he was a young man he was famous throughout the province for his courage and daring. Though he was small he was very handsome and many women fell in love with him. Conor decided it was time his nephew married. He was afraid the druid's prophecy would come true and he wanted Cuchulainn to leave a son after him who would grow up to be a hero like his father.

The king sent messengers all over Ireland to find a wife for his nephew. But though they searched for a year they failed to find a woman that suited him.

'There must be some girl you like!' the king said with a gesture of impatience.

'I haven't met her yet,' Cuchulainn said. 'But when I do I'll marry her.'

Then one day when he was out hunting he met Emer. She was the daughter of Forgall, chieftain of Lusk, and she was walking

near her father's fort when Cuchulainn's chariot sped by. He pulled the horses to a sudden stop, nearly overturning the chariot. He jumped out, strode over to her, and introduced himself.

'I have heard of your fame,' she smiled and told him who she was.

'And I have heard of your beauty,' Cuchulainn said. 'I see now that every word of it is true.'

They walked and talked for a while. Then Cuchulainn asked her to marry him.

'I will gladly be your wife,' Emer answered, 'but first you must talk to my father.'

'I'll talk to him now,' Cuchulainn said, turning towards the fort.

Emer shook her head. 'He is away at present. Come back in a week and you will find him here.'

'I shall do that,' Cuchulainn promised. He kissed her then, leaped into his chariot, and whipped up the horses. He turned as he drove away and waved to Emer. She waved back to him, her eyes glowing with love.

But Forgall was angry when he heard what had happened. As was the custom at the time, he had already promised his daughter in marriage to a wealthy nobleman. The last thing he wanted was to see her married to Cuchulainn. 'I'll soon put an end to this!' he swore.

He travelled in disguise to Eman Macha and went to see Cuchulainn. First he praised his heroism. Then he told him he could be an even better hero if he visited Scatha, the great woman warrior who lived far away in the Land of Shadows.

'If you study with her,' Forgall said, 'you will become the greatest hero in the world.'

He smiled persuasively as he spoke. He knew that the Land of Shadows was full of danger and that Cuchulainn might never return alive.

Cuchulainn hesitated, then nodded his head. 'I will go and visit Scatha,' he said.

Forgall returned triumphantly to his fort. He called Emer and told her what he had done. 'You will never see Cuchulainn again,' he laughed.

But before he left Ireland, Cuchulainn arranged to meet Emer in secret. She told him of her father's trickery. 'You must be very careful,' she warned. 'He will do his best to destroy you.'

They promised to be faithful to each other. Then Cuchulainn set out for the Land of Shadows. After long travelling he arrived at the camp where Scatha's pupils lived. He asked where Scatha was and they told him she was on an island nearby. It could only be reached by the Pupils' Bridge. 'But no one can cross it,' they said, 'unless he is a fully-trained warrior; for the bridge is low at each end and high in the centre, and if you step on one end the other end flies up and throws you down.'

Cuchulainn made three attempts to cross the bridge. He failed every time. The others began to jeer him. This angered Cuchulainn.

He approached the bridge again, crouched down, and prepared to make a great salmon leap. He hurled himself into the air and landed in the centre of the bridge. Then he sprang up quickly again and reached the island safely. He went to Scatha's fort and hammered on the door with his spear.

Scatha gave him a great welcome. He stayed with her for a

year and a day, learning all the heroic skills she had.

'You are the best pupil I have ever trained,' she said with a pleased expression on her face. 'Before you go home I will give you a special weapon called the Ga Bolga.' The Ga was a spear that was thrown with the foot. When it pierced an enemy it filled every part of his body with its barbs.

Then, his training finished, Cuchulainn returned to Ireland and to Emer. But his troubles with her father were not over yet.

CHAPTER SIX
The Enchanted Land of the Shee

ON THE JOURNEY BACK TO IRELAND Cuchulainn thought only of his coming reunion with Emer. He could hardly wait to see her again.

Immediately the boat touched land he leaped into his chariot and drove directly towards Forgall's fort. He cracked his whip impatiently over the horses' heads, urging them on to greater speed. The wheels of the chariot carved deep ruts in the rough track, sending clouds of dust billowing high in the air. Soon the fort came into view and Cuchulainn gave a great shout of delight. The sound echoed for miles around, alarming the birds and animals of the countryside.

But it also alarmed Forgall inside the fort. He looked out, saw Cuchulainn approaching, and ordered his guards to lock the gate. Then, taking Emer by the arm, he hurried with her to the top of the highest tower in the fort. Cuchulainn pulled his horses to a

halt in front of the gate and jumped out of the chariot.

'Emer!' he called out. Emer tried to answer him but her father clasped his hand over her mouth. Cuchulainn ran up to the massive wooden gate and knocked on it loudly.

The gate did not open. He knocked on it again. But it still did not open. Then he beat a tattoo on the gate with the shaft of his spear. 'Go away!' a rough voice ordered.

Cuchulainn hesitated, then turned and walked slowly away. Forgall laughed triumphantly as he watched from the tower.

'The young pup is leaving,' he whispered in Emer's ear. 'He will bother us no more.' Her brown eyes clouded with tears.

Then Cuchulainn stopped, spun around, and faced the fort. He dropped into a crouch and the muscles of his body began to ripple like waves in the sea. Suddenly he launched himself into his salmon leap. He soared like an arrow high over the walls of the fort and landed in the centre of the courtyard.

'Kill him!' Forgall shouted angrily to his men. Twelve guards rushed into the courtyard and trapped Cuchulainn inside a bristling circle of spears. He quickly drew his sword and with swift flashing strokes cut down six of the guards. The others retreated, then threw away their weapons and fled.

'Emer!' Cuchulainn called out again. Emer suddenly broke free from her father's grip and raced down to the door of the tower. As soon as she appeared in the doorway Cuchulainn ran over to her. But Forgall thought he was coming to kill him and he made a desperate attempt to escape by climbing down the outside of the tower. His foot slipped and he plunged to his death on the ground below.

More guards rushed out to attack Cuchulainn. He took Emer in his arms and prepared to make his salmon leap again. Before the guards could reach them Cuchulainn and Emer shot up in the air and flew back over the walls of the fort, landing beside the chariot. He leaped into the chariot, pulled Emer in quickly, and soon they were speeding away in the direction of Eman Macha.

But they were not yet out of danger. A hundred of Forgall's men chased them on horseback and gradually caught up with them. Cuchulainn suddenly wheeled the chariot around and drove through his pursuers. They were mown down by the razor-sharp knives fixed to the wheels of the chariot.

Then Cuchulainn turned the chariot around again and drove to Eman Macha. Conor and his nobles gave them a great welcome when they arrived at the palace.

'This is my future wife,' Cuchulainn said, presenting Emer to the king.

'You have made an excellent choice!' the king smiled. Soon afterwards they were married and there was feasting and music and dancing until dawn in the huge hall of the palace.

Cuchulainn and Emer went to live in his house at Dun Dealgan. They were very happy there and their love for each other grew stronger with every year that passed. Then one day something very strange happened.

Cuchulainn had gone hunting deer with two companions. They came upon a stag in a wood. It was a magnificent-looking animal with wide towering antlers branching from its head. Cuchulainn's eyes gleamed when he saw it. 'This will make a fine prize,' he whispered to his companions.

The animal bounded away and they immediately gave chase. Although Cuchulainn could outrun most animals the stag was

swifter than him. They chased it all day but could not get close
to it. Then the stag led them into a narrow valley in the mountains
and stopped. Cuchulainn ran up and raised his spear. The stag
suddenly vanished right in front of his eyes. He stared around in
astonishment. His companions joined him, panting for breath
after the long chase.

'Where is the stag?' one of them asked.

'I don't know,' Cuchulainn replied in a puzzled voice. 'It just
disappeared into thin air.'

The sun descended behind the mountains and it grew dark.
Stars began to shimmer in the inky sky. One of his companions
shivered and said, 'I don't like this place. Let's go home.'

Cuchulainn shook his head. 'It is too late for that,' he said.
'We'll rest here for the night.'

So they settled down to sleep. But during the night Cuchulainn
had a strange dream. Two banshees came to him, one dressed in
a cloak of green, the other in a cloak of red. They beat him with
rods and then disappeared. When Cuchulainn woke up in the
morning he felt very sick and weak. He tried to rise but fell down
like a helpless baby. His companions were alarmed when they
saw the state he was in.

'We had better take you home to Emer,' one said. The other
nodded his head in agreement.

'No, I don't want to worry her,' Cuchulainn whispered. 'Bring
me to Eman Macha. The druids there will cure me of this strange
illness.'

So they carried him to the palace at Eman Macha. The druids
tried all their remedies and spells but none of them cured
Cuchulainn. He lay there for weeks hardly able to move. Then
one day a stranger in a green cloak came to see him.

'Return to the place where you had the dream,' he told Cuchulainn, 'and you will regain your strength.' As the stranger turned to leave Cuchulainn saw that he had a picture of a stag's head embroidered on the back of his cloak.

Cuchulainn sent for Laeg his charioteer and ordered him to take him to the place of the dream. Then he told Laeg to put him sitting on the ground and to leave him there alone. The charioteer had just driven out of sight when the banshee in the red cloak appeared at Cuchulainn's side.

'Who are you?' he asked.

'I have been sent here by Fann, Queen of the Land of the Shee,' she replied. 'Three evil kings are attacking her country. She needs your help.'

'Can her husband, the great Mananaan Mac Lir, not help her?' Cuchulainn asked.

'They have quarrelled and he has left her,' the banshee explained. 'You must come to her aid.'

'I am in no fit state to do battle with anyone,' Cuchulainn declared.

'You will soon be better and as strong as ever,' the banshee said, 'if you promise to come and help Fann.'

Cuchulainn hesitated. He wanted to remain in Ireland with Emer. But he also wanted to regain his strength.

'Well?' the banshee demanded. 'Have you made up your mind?'

'Yes,' Cuchulainn answered. 'I promise I will come to the Land of the Shee. Provided I am first allowed to send my charioteer there to see what it is like.'

'Very well,' the banshee agreed. She then spread her cloak between them and disappeared. Soon afterwards Cuchulainn felt his strength surging back into his body.

He jumped to his feet, ran swiftly after Laeg, and caught up with the charioteer before he had time to arrive at Eman Macha. He told Laeg to go at once to the Land of the Shee to see what it was like.

Cuchulainn then hurried home to Emer and explained what had happened to him.

'Do not visit the land of Fann,' she pleaded. 'I am afraid some evil will befall you there.'

'But I have given my solemn promise.'

'Even so. Stay here with me.'

'I will decide what to do when I hear what Laeg has to say,' Cuchulainn said.

When Laeg returned from the Land of the Shee he was full of its praises. 'Nowhere else have I seen such a beautiful place,' he declared. 'I would gladly go back and stay there for the rest of my life.'

'And this woman, Fann?' Cuchulainn enquired. 'What is she like?'

'She is tall and fair and very lovely. In fact she is the loveliest woman I have ever seen,' Laeg replied. 'Except for Emer,' he added.

'Did she give you any message for me?'

Laeg nodded. 'She told me to remind you of your promise and that you must go to her soon.'

Cuchulainn sent the charioteer home and sat down to think about what he would do. He was reluctant to leave Emer but he was afraid of losing his strength again if he failed to keep his promise. Finally he made up his mind. He strode into the orchard where Emer was resting in the shade of a tree.

'I have decided to go to the Land of the Shee,' he announced.

'I am sad that you are leaving me,' Emer said softly.

Cuchulainn smiled at her reassuringly. 'Do not worry,' he said. 'I shall not be long away.'

Emer reached out and took his hand. 'I'll make certain of that,' she said solemnly. 'I now put a *geas* on you - you must promise to return to me within a month.'

'There is no need to put such a spell on me!' he laughed. 'I will come back long before then.'

So Cuchulainn went away to the Land of the Shee. It was every bit as wonderful as Laeg had described. And Fann was as beautiful as he had said. Cuchulainn was enchanted by the tall graceful queen and immediately fell in love with her.

'I am very glad you have come,' Fann said, her deep green eyes returning his love. 'And now that you are strong again you must help me defeat my enemies.'

Then Cuchulainn went out to do battle with the three evil kings. Although they were full of cunning and treachery he defeated them and cut off their heads. He hurried back to Fann and announced that her enemies were dead.

'You have done well,' she smiled. 'Now I will show you my gratitude. You will stay here with me and forget all about the land you came from.'

So Cuchulainn stayed with Fann. Weeks went by and he forgot about Emer. But just before the month was up the *geas* took effect and he remembered her again. He explained to Fann that he had to return home because of the *geas*. But he promised to meet her again in Ireland on the Strand of the Yew Tree near his home.

Emer's face lit up with joy when Cuchulainn returned. But after a while she sensed that something was wrong.

'You have changed,' she complained. 'You do not love me any more.'

'That is not true!' Cuchulainn protested.

Emer shook her head doubtfully and went out to sit under her favourite tree. She sat there wondering about the change that had come over Cuchulainn. The tree suddenly whispered to her that Cuchulainn was in love with Fann and had promised to meet her again.

So when Cuchulainn set out for the Strand of the Yew Tree Emer followed him with seven of her servants. On her instructions they carried long sharp knives. Emer was determined to deal with her rival ... even if it meant having to kill her!

She watched jealously as Cuchulainn took Fann into his chariot and embraced her. 'Slay that woman!' she ordered. The servants advanced on the chariot, brandishing their knives. Fann glanced over Cuchulainn's shoulder and saw them. She began to tremble with fear.

'What is troubling you?' he asked.

'Look! Those women are coming to kill me!'

Cuchulainn turned and leaped out of the chariot. Then, standing in front of Emer and her servants he demanded, 'Why are you doing this?'

'Because she wants to take you from me,' Emer replied, here eyes flashing with hate as she pointed at Fann.

'I love her ...' Cuchulainn began to say but Emer cut him short.

'You loved me too. Once we lived in honour together and you looked on me with favour.'

'I still do,' Cuchulainn said.

When Fann heard this she started weeping bitterly. Her husband Mananaan heard her as she wept. He came to her, covered in his magic cloak which made him invisible to all but Fann.

'Will you come with me or stay with Cuchulainn?' he asked her.

'I will go with you', Fann replied sadly, 'for Cuchulainn already has a woman who is worthy of him.' And so she went away with Mananaan.

But Cuchulainn was still enchanted by Fann and when he saw her leaving him he ran into the mountains and wandered there for days touching neither food nor drink.

Emer went to Eman Macha and told King Conor what had happened. He immediately sent his druids out to find Cuchulainn and cure him. After much searching they found him and gave him a magic potion which made him forget Fann completely. They then gave the same drink to Emer so that she also forgot her.

Then Cuchulainn and Emer returned to their home in Dun Dealgan and lived there happily together. And nothing came between them and their love for each other ever again.

'And that is the story of Cuchulainn,' Fergus said to Maeve. The queen gave a disdainful laugh. 'This hero it seems is human after all,' she declared. 'We will sweep him out of our way!'

But that was not to prove as easy as she thought.

CHAPTER SEVEN

Death of Maeve's Son

HIDDEN ON A NEARBY HILL, Cuchulainn watched with a smile on his lips as four of Maeve's strongest warriors tried to remove the tree fork from the middle of the ford. They heaved and pulled but failed to budge it one inch.

'Leave it!' the queen ordered with an impatient gesture. 'We will try and drive our chariots around it.'

But no chariot succeeded in passing the tree fork and thirty of them were smashed in the attempt. Maeve seethed with anger as she surveyed the damage.

'Repair those chariots,' she commanded. 'We'll make camp here in the meantime and find another way across the river tomorrow.'

Cuchulainn lay down to rest. He knew his best plan was to keep delaying Maeve's army until Conor and his men woke up from their enchanted sleep in Eman Macha.

Suddenly he heard the sound of a tree being cut down in a wood at the foot of the hill. He hurried into the wood and discovered a young charioteer wielding an axe. The charioteer whirled in alarm as a twig cracked under Cuchulainn's foot. A look of relief came over his face when he saw that the intruder was a small man not much older than himself.

'Help me cut these wood shafts,' he said to Cuchulainn. 'We smashed most of our chariots because of that wild fox Cuchulainn.'

'Shall I gather the shafts or trim them?' Cuchulainn asked.

'I'll do the gathering since that's the easiest part of it,' the charioteer grinned. He watched as Cuchulainn picked up some tree shafts. 'You'll need a knife to trim them,' he said.

Cuchulainn shook his head and quickly pulled the shafts through his hands and feet leaving them clean and polished. The charioteer stared at him in astonishment.

'Who are you?' he asked in a puzzled voice.

'I'm that Cuchulainn you were talking about.'

The charioteer's eyes glinted with sudden fear. 'Th... this is the end of me !' he stammered.

'Who are you?' Cuchulainn enquired.

'I'm the charioteer of Orlam, Maeve's son.' The man began to tremble.

'Don't be afraid,' Cuchulainn said. 'I never kill drivers or messengers.' He paused and then asked, 'Where is your master?''

'He's waiting for me at the edge of the wood,' the charioteer replied.

'Stay here,' Cuchulainn ordered, and he raced off to where Orlam was waiting. Orlam drew his sword when he saw Cuchulainn coming but Cuchulainn knocked it from his hand and cut off his head. Then he returned to the charioteer and placed the head on his back.

'Take this to Maeve exactly as it is,' he commanded. 'Tell her there is worse to come if she doesn't turn back.'

The charioteer went straight to Maeve and delivered the message. For a moment she was speechless with fury. Then at the top of her voice she screeched, 'I shall have revenge on this pup for the death of my son!'

Cuchulainn heard her back on the hill and, taking careful aim with his sling-shot, fired a stone at her head. The stone killed the pet bird perched on her shoulder. Her bodyguards rushed over

and put a covering of shields above her head.

'Perhaps it would be best to go back after all,' Fergus suggested.

'No!' Maeve snapped. 'We will continue on to Cooley. And we'll kill Cuchulainn the first chance we get!'

CHAPTER EIGHT

Cuchulainn Fights the Great Warrior of Munster

THOUGH MAEVE'S ARMY SUCCEEDED in crossing the river they did not get very far. Cuchulainn harassed them every day, killing many warriors with his sling-shot. Finally, in desperation, Maeve decided to play a trick on him.

She sent part of her army in one direction, guessing that Cuchulainn would follow them. Then, when the way was clear, she headed straight for Cooley with the rest of the army.

'Now', she smiled when they came in sight of Cooley, 'the Brown Bull will soon be mine.'

Daire Mac Fiachna was sitting down to breakfast when a servant burst into the room. He told Daire that the army of Connacht was approaching. Daire jumped up, his fat jowls quivering with excitement.

'We must hide the bull on Slieve Cuilinn,' he said. 'Get him away as quickly as you can!'

So the Brown Bull was hurried away. Daire followed in his chariot. He had just disappeared out of sight when Maeve's men

arrived at his house. They searched everywhere and then reported to Maeve that the bull was gone.

She ground her teeth in anger and sent for her herdsman.

'Where do you think the animal is hidden?' she asked.

'Most likely on Slieve Cuilinn,' he answered.

'Take some men,' she ordered. 'Find the bull and bring it here.'

The men went off and came upon the bull hidden in a glen. They drove Daire and his servant away and brought the bull back to Maeve's camp. But it broke free and ran bellowing through the camp killing fifty of the queen's warriors. Then it disappeared into the mountains and though they searched far and wide the Connachtmen failed to find it.

Cuchulainn meanwhile had discovered the trick that Maeve had played on him. Furious at the deception, he turned in his tracks and sped after the other part of her army. They were sitting round their fires talking and laughing when Cuchulainn announced his arrival. Stones from his sling-shot whistled through the camp killing a hundred warriors. Men ran here and there in panic.

Maeve decided to change her tactics. She sent a messenger to Cuchulainn offering him a quarter of her wealth if he stopped attacking her.

Cuchulainn immediately refused the offer. 'Go back and tell your queen that I am not to be bought,' he said in a voice full of contempt.

'Will you come and meet her and Fergus?' the messenger asked.

Cuchulainn hesitated and then agreed. Though he had no great wish to see the queen he welcomed the chance to meet his foster-father again.

Maeve's eyes narrowed as she watched him approaching the camp. 'I'm amazed to see how young and small he is,' she said to Fergus.

'Even though he's so young and small no man can conquer him in single combat,' Fergus said quietly.

Cuchulainn embraced his foster-father, then turned to Maeve. 'You wish to talk to me?' he said coolly.

'Yes,' she replied. 'I will give you half my wealth if you will give up this foolish fight.'

Cuchulainn shook his head, turned on his heel, and walked away. For the next three days and nights his sling-shot continued to terrify the queen's camp. Maeve was at her wits' end.

'What terms will this man accept from me?' she asked Fergus.

'I think the only terms he will agree to is to fight your warriors one by one,' Fergus replied.

Maeve thought briefly about this. Then she shrugged and said: 'I prefer to lose one man every day than a hundred every night. Go and tell him what is proposed.' Fergus got into his chariot. Just then he saw that Maeve's foster-son, Edarcomal, was preparing to come with him.

'You had better stay here,' he said.

'Why?' Edarcomal demanded.

'I'm afraid of you starting a fight with Cuchulainn,' Fergus said. 'You're so proud and overbearing that there's sure to be trouble between the pair of you.'

'If that's what's worrying you put me under your protection,' Edarcomal suggested.

'Very well,' Fergus agreed. 'But take care not to force him into

a fight.'

When they drove out in their chariots to where Cuchulainn was resting, Fergus explained that Edarcomal was under his protection. He went on then to tell of Maeve's proposal. When Cuchulainn agreed to this Fergus returned to the camp. Edarcomal followed him part of the way, then suddenly turned his chariot towards Cuchulainn, signalling he wanted combat. But Cuchulainn shook his head.

'You are afraid of me,' Edarcomal called out jeeringly. When he heard this Cuchulainn drew his sword and rushed at him. Edarcomal leaped from his chariot and raised his sword. But Cuchulainn swiftly cut the ground from under his feet so that he fell flat on his back.

'Go away now,' Cuchulainn said. 'Only for Fergus I'd have cut you in two.'

Edarcomal jumped to his feet. 'I won't leave here until I take your head with me!' he shouted.

'Let it be so then,' Cuchulainn said. With a flick of his sword he sliced all the hair off Edarcomal's head without shedding a drop of blood.

'Go off now,' he said, 'because I've made a laughing-stock of you.'

Edarcomal attacked him furiously. But Cuchulainn's sword flashed like lightning, slicing off his opponent's clothes so that they fell down leaving him untouched. Still Edarcomal attacked and in the heat of the fight Cuchulainn split his skull with a blow. Edarcomal fell dead to the ground.

When Fergus saw what happened he drove back to Cuchulainn.

'Why did you do that to one who came here under my

protection?' he demanded angrily.

'I didn't cause this fight,' Cuchulainn explained. 'He wouldn't leave unless he took my head with him. He left me no choice.'

'Well, he's paid the price of his arrogance,' Fergus said. He put Edarcomal's body in his chariot and brought it back to the camp. Maeve stared at the body of her foster-son.

'I thought he was under your protection,' she said bitterly.

'The whelp attacked the Great Hound of Culann,' Fergus replied. 'Even I would be lucky to survive an encounter with him!'

'I will find an opponent to match this demon!' the queen declared.

'Who?'

'Nodcrandal, the greatest warrior in Munster.'

'But he has already refused to help you. He will hardly come now.'

'Yes, he will,' Maeve said confidently, 'when he hears what I have to offer him.'

She sent a message to Nodcrandal promising him her daughter in marriage if he would come and fight Cuchulainn. Nodcrandal agreed immediately. He jumped into his chariot and drove straight to Maeve's camp. The queen greeted him warmly. He was a tall powerful man with a curly black beard that covered most of his face.

'Where is this Cuchulainn?' he demanded in a fierce booming voice.

Maeve indicated a hill in front of the camp. 'You will find him there,' she said.

Nodcrandal turned to set off for the hill. 'You are forgetting your weapons,' the queen reminded him.

'I will make some spears of holly,' Nodcrandal said. 'That is all I need to kill this pup.'

On his way up the hill he cut seven spears of holly and whittled them to razor-sharp points. Then he marched to the top of the hill and saw Cuchulainn before him hunting birds.

'This is the last time you will go hunting, little man,' he growled and suddenly threw the spears. Cuchulainn heard them whizzing through the air and with a deer-like bound leaped from one spear point to another until he stood on the point of the last spear. Then he sped after the birds for he depended on them for food during the *Táin*.

When Nodcrandal saw this he thought Cuchulainn was fleeing from him. He laughed and swaggered back to the camp. 'This great hero you talk about has run away from me,' he announced boastfully.

'I knew he would,' Maeve said. 'He's frightened of a real warrior like you.'

But when Fergus heard this he shook his head sadly. He was ashamed it should be said that one man could make Cuchulainn run away. He called one of his messengers. 'Tell Cuchulainn he should go now and hide since he has fled from one man. He shames all the men of Ulster as well as himself.'

The messenger went and told this to Cuchulainn.

'Who is boasting of that among you?' Cuchulainn asked.

'Nodcrandal,' the messenger replied.

'He wouldn't be boasting now if he'd had real weapons in his hands,' Cuchulainn said. 'All he carried were branches of holly. Fergus knows that I don't kill unarmed men.' He paused an instant. 'Tell Nodcrandal to come again tomorrow. I'll be waiting for him and I won't run away.'

The messenger returned to the camp and told Nodcrandal what Cuchulainn had said. Nodcrandal snorted in derision. 'I shall meet the whelp tomorrow and put an end to him!' he swore.

Early next morning Nodcrandal set out in his chariot to fight Cuchulainn. This time he carried all his weapons. But when Cuchulainn appeared Nodcrandal began to mock him because he had no beard.

'I can't take a little lamb's head back to camp,' he jeered.

'Wait here,' Cuchulainn said. 'I'll be back.'

He ran up the hill and gathered two handfuls of moss. Then he dyed it with blackberry juice and stuck it on his chin. He raced back to Nodcrandal and said, 'Now, let us fight.'

'First we must settle the rules of combat,' Nodcrandal declared.

'Name them yourself,' Cuchulainn said.

Nodcrandal smiled craftily. 'You must agree not to dodge my spear when I throw it at you.'

Cuchulainn nodded. Nodcrandal suddenly threw a spear at him but Cuchulainn evaded it by jumping up high.

'You have cheated by dodging my spear,' Nodcrandal complained.

'You can dodge my spear the same way,' Cuchulainn said.

Nodcrandal prepared to jump as Cuchulainn threw the weapon. But Cuchulainn launched it upwards so that it landed on Nodcrandal's skull. Nodcrandal bellowed with anger and flung his sword at Cuchulainn. With a great leap Cuchulainn came down on the rim of Nodcrandal's shield, balanced there an instant, and then cut off his head.

He flung it into the middle of Maeve's camp. It landed at the queen's feet. An expression of fury came over her face. She shook her fist at the hill where Cuchulainn lay resting. 'I will defeat you yet!' she shouted.

Then she turned and stormed into her tent.

CHAPTER NINE
Morrigan

MAEVE SAT A LONG TIME IN HER TENT considering what she should do about Cuchulainn. He had killed many men in her army. And she knew he would kill many more unless she could find a way to stop him. But what worried her most was that she had still failed to capture the Brown Bull of Cooley.

Something must be done! But what? She thought of asking her druid to cast a spell on Cuchulainn. But then she remembered that he had been unaffected by the enchanted sleep put on the men at Eman Macha. Her nostrils twitched with annoyance. His godfather, the great Lug of the Long Arm, probably protected him from magic spells! She racked her brains trying to think of some weakness in her enemy.

Suddenly she smiled. She had just recalled Fergus's story about Cuchulainn and Fann. Perhaps he could be distracted again by a beautiful woman. She thought of her daughter, then shook her head. No, Cuchulainn would immediately be suspicious. This required more subtle trickery. She smiled again. Who was better for the task than her old friend Morrigan the Witch?

Morrigan, she knew, could change herself into any form. She would ask her to turn herself into a very beautiful woman and go to Cuchulainn.

The queen sent a messenger at once to Morrigan. The witch cackled gleefully when she heard the plan. She had hated Cuchulainn for a long while and was glad of this chance to trick him while helping her royal friend at the same time.

'Tell the queen I shall go this very evening to see Cuchulainn,' she said.

That evening Maeve and her army set out once more in search of the Brown Bull. Cuchulainn watched from a nearby hill and got ready to attack them.

A beautiful young woman suddenly appeared at his side. She was tall and noble-looking and wore a long glittering cloak of gold. He gazed at her in astonishment.

'Who are you?' he asked

'I am King Buan's daughter,' she replied, 'and I have loved you for a very long time.'

'Go away!' Cuchulainn ordered. 'I have important business to look after here.'

'Come with me and I will give you all my treasures and cattle,' the woman said.

'No,' Cuchulainn said impatiently. 'I told you I am busy.'

'You'll regret it if you don't come,' the woman warned.

'Can't you see I'm preparing for combat?' Cuchulainn said, gesturing at the army which was rapidly disappearing out of sight. 'My enemies are escaping.'

'I will be your enemy too,' the woman said, 'if you don't do as I say. I'll hinder you in battle. When you are fighting in the ford I'll come in the shape of an eel and trip you up.'

Cuchulainn stared at her angrily. 'You are no king's daughter!' he shouted. 'I think you are a witch!'

The woman changed suddenly into a snake. Its tongue flickered venomously at Cuchulainn. He drew his sword and aimed a blow at its head. But the snake changed instantly into a raven and with a harsh croak flew quickly away.

Cuchulainn raced after Maeve's army. But before he caught up with them some slipped away and found where the Brown Bull was hiding. They captured the bull and drove it back towards the rest of the army. Cuchulainn saw them coming and attacked them fiercely. In the fury of battle he failed to notice that a small group of soldiers was escaping with the bull. They hurried as fast as they could back to Maeve.

The queen's eyes glowed with delight when she saw the Brown Bull. 'Take it to Cruachan immediately!' she ordered her herdsman. 'We will make camp at this ford and stop Cuchulainn from following you.'

Cuchulainn was furious when he discovered the bull was gone. He raced like the wind back to Maeve's camp and at once began to attack it. The queen sent warriors out one by one to fight them but Cuchulainn killed them all. Then she sent twenty men at a time against him but Cuchulainn killed them too. Worried by the rapid slaughter of her warriors she decided that single combat was best after all. So she ordered the warrior Cuar Mac Daluat out to do battle.

Cuar was the most unpopular man in the camp. He was cranky and disagreeable and nobody liked to sit near him at meals. But he was a good warrior and when he drew blood from a man, that man died within a week.

'If he kills Cuchulainn our troubles are over,' Maeve observed. 'And even if he is killed himself it will be no great loss.'

When Cuar arrived at the ford, Cuchulainn was eating an apple. Cuar hammered on his shield with a spear. Cuchulainn ignored him and went on eating the apple. Cuar threw the spear but it missed. Cuchulainn turned slowly and flung the apple at his head. It cracked Cuar's skull and he died on the spot.

Maeve then sent for Ferbet who had been one of Cuchulainn's comrades at the school in Eman Macha.

'You were trained with Cuchulainn,' Maeve said. 'You should know all his tricks. Go out there and fight him.'

'I do not wish to fight an old friend,' Ferbet said.

'I'll give you my daughter in marriage if you go out and kill him,' Maeve offered.

'Very well,' Ferbet said. 'I agree.'

He went out to meet Cuchulainn. But Cuchulainn was reluctant to do battle with him. 'We are old comrades,' he said. 'Let's call off this fight.'

Ferbet shook his head. 'I can't,' he said. 'I've given Maeve my promise.'

'Keep your friendship then!' Cuchulainn exclaimed angrily. He turned and went back. But on the way a large splinter of holly pierced the sole of his foot. He pulled it out impatiently and threw it over his shoulder. The splinter soared through the air and embedded itself in Ferbet's head. He fell dead where he was.

When Maeve's warriors saw this most of them refused to do single combat with Cuchulainn. So the queen decided to use some trickery. She sent for a rash young warrior called Lairine Mac Nesh. She gave him a lot of wine to drink and then offered him her daughter if he brought in Cuchulainn's head. Lairine agreed at once. But his only brother Lugad, King of Munster, heard of Maeve's trickery and became alarmed. He went to see Cuchulainn.

'Don't kill Lairine and leave me brotherless,' he pleaded.

Cuchulainn nodded his head. 'I won't kill him', he promised, 'but he might be better off dead after I've dealt with him.'

Next morning Lairine went out to do battle with Cuchulainn.

He was astonished when Cuchulainn confronted him un-armed. 'Where are your weapons?' he asked.

Cuchulainn smiled and said, 'I don't need any to deal with you.'

Lairine's mouth twisted in anger. 'You'll be sorry for that insult!' he roared. With flailing sword he advanced on Cuchulainn. As he came within reach, Cuchulainn grabbed his wrists in a vice-like grip. He shook Lairine furiously and the sword flew out of the warrior's hands. Then he caught him around the ribs in a crushing hold and shook him like a doll. Finally he flung him back into the camp where he landed in his brother's arms.

From that day on Lairine had difficulty eating and could not lie down without pain. But he could count himself lucky to have survived after a fight with Cuchulainn. For he was the only man to do so in the *Táin*.

Maeve then asked a Leinster warrior called Loch to do battle with Cuchulainn. He shook his head in refusal.

'I won't fight a beardless youth,' he declared. 'But', he added, 'my brother Long is willing to go out.'

But when Long went out to fight, Cuchulainn killed him with his sword. His body was carried back to the camp. Loch screamed in anger when he saw his dead brother.

'If a bearded man had done this I'd make him pay dearly for it!' he shouted.

Cuchulainn heard his words, put on another false beard, and appeared in front of the camp.

'Look!' Maeve said. 'Cuchulainn has a beard.' She turned to Loch. 'It is fitting that you fight him now.'

So Loch went out to do battle with Cuchulainn. They met in the middle of the ford.

'Now I'll avenge my brother!' Loch hissed and raising his sword with both hands he aimed a vicious blow at Cuchulainn's head. Cuchulainn warded off the blow with the side of his sword.

Then, standing toe to toe, they flailed away at each other so that sparks flew from the clashing steel. A long eel suddenly appeared in the ford. It swam up to Cuchulainn and flung its coils around his feet. He tripped and fell down in the ford. Morrigan had carried out her threat!

When Loch saw Cuchulainn falling back he attacked him savagely, wounding him so badly that the ford was red with blood.

But Laeg was watching from the river bank and he sent the Ga Bolga gliding down the stream. Cuchulainn caught it with his toe and flicked it into Loch's body. Loch stood swaying for an instant in the middle of the ford.

'Move back and let me fall on my face,' he said. 'If I fall on my back they'll say I was running away from you.'

Cuchulainn moved back and Loch fell forward on his face,

dead. Then Cuchulainn attacked the eel but it swam away and wriggled up on the river bank. Cuchulainn followed it with sword poised to strike. The eel changed immediately into a wolf and came at him with snapping fangs but Cuchulainn struck it on the eye and it fled into the hills howling with pain.

A great tiredness suddenly came over Cuchulainn. His wounds had weakened him and he was weary from fighting Maeve's warriors on his own. He called Laeg and asked him to go to Eman

Macha to try and wake up the Ulstermen. But Laeg refused to leave him.

'I am thirsty,' Cuchulainn whispered and he lay on the ground. His charioteer brought him water from the river. He gulped it down and stretched out to rest.

Maeve's eyes gleamed with triumph when she saw Cuchulainn lying on the river bank. 'Attack the pup now!' she urged the warriors around her. 'He is too weak to fight.'

A group of them went out at once against Cuchulainn.

'Maeve's men are coming!' Laeg warned.

Cuchulainn rose, went down to the ford, and killed all the warriors that came against him. Then he walked slowly back and made for a nearby hill to rest for the night.

He was gripped again by a raging thirst. Suddenly Morrigan appeared before him in the shape of a one-eyed old woman. She was milking a cow and Cuchulainn asked her for a drink. She nodded smilingly and gave him milk from the cow.

Cuchulainn drank it and turned to thank her. 'May the gods bless the giver!' he said. The hag's missing eye was immediately restored. He stared at her in astonishment.

'You are that witch!' he exclaimed.

'And the eel and the wolf,' she cackled. 'Your blessing has healed my eye.'

'I am sorry I gave it to you,' Cuchulainn said.

'You will be even sorrier before the *Táin* is over,' she laughed. And changing into a raven she flew away.

CHAPTER TEN

The Boy-troop of Eman Macha

THAT EVENING CUCHULAINN RESTED ON A HILL looking down on Maeve's camp. The rows of tents stretched into the distance as far as his eyes could see. The weapons stacked outside glittered in the sunset and dazzled him with their brilliance.

He sighed as he realised how numerous his enemies still were. His wounds stung him and his body ached for sleep. But he knew he dared not sleep. That was the opportunity Maeve and her men were waiting for. He must stay awake!

A sudden rage came over him and he rose and took up his weapons. He rattled them angrily and shouted his fierce battle-cry. The demons of the air answered his shout so that a terrifying noise pierced the sky. A hush fell over the camp below as Maeve and her warriors heard it.

But someone else had heard it too. It woke him from his sleep in a cave in the mountains. He reached for his magic stone and gazed into it. He shook his head as he saw the exhausted expression on Cuchulainn's face and the wounds that covered his body. His godson was in trouble! Lug of the Long Arm got quickly to his feet, put on his green cloak, and took his huge sword and long forked spear in his hands. Then he strode out of the cave and went in search of Cuchulainn.

The ground trembled under his giant steps as he approached the hill. Cuchulainn's drooping eyes suddenly opened wide when he saw him coming. He gave a whoop of delight and ran to welcome his godfather.

They sat down by the fire. A worried frown came over Lug's

face as he looked at Cuchulainn. 'You are badly wounded,' he said.

Cuchulainn nodded. 'And very tired too,' he said. 'I have been standing alone against the might of four provinces.'

'I will help you, my son,' Lug said quietly. 'You must lie down now and sleep. But first I will heal your wounds.'

He opened the pouch on his belt and took out some magic herbs. Then he put them on Cuchulainn's wounds and they were immediately healed. 'Sleep now,' he said. 'I shall watch over you.'

'But who will defend the ford?' Cuchulainn asked anxiously.

'I will summon the boy-troop from the school at Eman Macha,' Lug replied. 'Because they are so young the sleeping spell has had no effect on them.'

He sang a soft lullaby to Cuchulainn who instantly fell into a deep sleep. He then caught a bird, tied a message to its leg, and sent it winging away to the school at Eman Macha.

Next morning, while Cuchulainn slept soundly, the boy-troop arrived at the ford. The only weapons they carried were their hurley-sticks. When Maeve saw them coming she sent for Fergus.

'Who are those children?' she asked.

'They're the boy-troop of Ulster,' Fergus replied. 'They've come to help Cuchulainn.'

Maeve laughed maliciously. 'He must be very weak if he's depending on children to help him!' she said. 'This is the chance we've been waiting for.' She turned and ordered a hundred warriors to go out and attack the ford.

The battle lasted for three days. Though the boy-troop fought bravely all of them were killed. But most of the warriors also died in the battle and the survivors staggered back to the camp to have their wounds looked after.

On the fourth morning Cuchulainn awoke. He felt refreshed and strong again. He stared up at Lug who was standing beside him resting on his great forked spear.

'How long have I slept?' he asked.

'Three days and three nights.'

'Has the boy-troop defended the ford?'

'Yes, but they all perished in the battle,' Lug replied, shaking his head sadly.

A low moaning sigh escaped from Cuchulainn's lips. 'If I had been there they wouldn't have died,' he said bitterly.

'You have nothing to be ashamed of,' Lug assured him. 'You had no choice but to rest.'

Cuchulainn jumped to his feet. 'Maeve and her army will pay dearly for this!' he vowed angrily. 'Stay with me,' he urged his godfather. 'We'll avenge the boy-troop together.'

Lug shook his head. 'Your enemies would think you were still too weak to fight your own battles. You are strong once again and able to do your own great deeds. I must return now to the Tuatha De Danaan.'

He smiled, raised his hand in farewell, and set off down the hill. The thunder of his footsteps gradually faded in the distance.

Cuchulainn called Laeg and ordered him to prepare the sickle chariot. Laeg hurried off and put battle-harness on the horses. Then he yoked them to the chariot. Its sides and wheels bristled with sharp blades and barbs that could tear an enemy into ribbons. When the sickle-chariot was ready Cuchulainn leaped into it and

grasped the reins.

A sudden battle-spasm ran through him and turned him into a strange distorted being that was terrifying to behold. His face and body swelled up with fury and his eyes glowed red like a blazing fire. He raised himself on the balls of his feet and shouted his loud ferocious war-cry. Then he drove the chariot straight at the camp below.

Maeve and her warriors came tumbling out of their tents. But before they could seize their weapons Cuchulainn was upon them. The warriors fell in their hundreds, cut to pieces by the whirring blades of the chariot. With terror-stricken eyes Maeve ran for her life and hid behind a bush. Men flew desperately in all directions trying to escape the death-dealing wheels.

But Cuchulainn was determined not to let them escape so easily. He turned the chariot and drove in a ring around the camp. The iron wheels bit deeply into the ground, throwing up a high circle of earth that trapped the men inside. Then he drove back into the middle of the camp leaving huge heaps of bodies behind him. Red streams of blood flowed over the plain and down into the river. Cuchulainn's lips moved in a grim smile. He wheeled his horses around and drove away.

For a short while an uncanny silence hung over the camp. Then Maeve emerged from her hiding-place and screeched with fury when she saw the slaughter. 'That demon has destroyed half my army!' she screamed.

'You were lucky not to lose all of it,' Fergus said.

'I must find some way to stop him,' Maeve said impatiently.

'Ask him for a truce,' Fergus suggested.

The queen nodded. 'Yes, tell him to meet me tomorrow to discuss a truce.' She paused and a cunning look came into her

eyes. 'And tell him to come unarmed.'

Fergus stared after her uneasily as she walked into her tent. He feared that Maeve was planning some treachery again.

CHAPTER ELEVEN
Fergus Confronts Cuchulainn

LAEG WAS VERY WORRIED when he heard that Cuchulainn had agreed to meet Maeve. 'Are you taking your weapons with you?' he asked.

Cuchulainn shook his head. 'I promised to go unarmed.'

An anxious frown creased Laeg's brow. 'Do you think that's wise?' he said. 'This queen is not to be trusted.'

'But she'll be unarmed too,' Cuchulainn said. He shrugged and added, 'Even if she's not she can do me no harm. She's not strong enough.'

'Still, she may be planning some bit of trickery,' Laeg warned. 'I'd bring a sword with me if I were you.'

'Very well,' Cuchulainn said. He buckled on his sword and set off for the meeting place. It was on a hill near the camp. Laeg's warning had alerted him and he glanced carefully around as he approached the hill. All seemed well. Maeve was alone and unarmed.

She smiled and raised her arm in greeting when he drew near. But the smile froze on her lips as soon as she saw the sword at his side.

'Why did you bring a weapon?' she asked icily.

Cuchulainn looked surprised and glanced down innocently at the sword. 'I'm sorry,' he apologised. 'I forgot to leave it behind me.'

'We can't discuss a truce while you're armed,' Maeve said. 'Put your sword on the ground.'

Cuchulainn unbuckled the weapon and threw it down beside him. Maeve immediately backed away from him and shouted 'Now!'

Fourteen of her warriors suddenly appeared from the other side of the hill and surrounded him with their spears. They hurled them at him just as he crouched down to grab his sword. The spears whistled harmlessly over his head. With swift thrusts of his sword Cuchulainn killed ten of his attackers. The rest fled with Maeve back to the safety of the camp.

Fergus was very angry when he heard how Maeve had tried to trick Cuchulainn. 'You must fight fair,' he warned her, 'or I will take my men away.'

The queen was silent for a moment. Fergus and his men were among the best warriors in her army and she had no wish to lose them. 'There will only be single combat with Cuchulainn from now on,' she promised.

For the next few days she sent out warriors one by one to fight Cuchulainn at the ford. But he defeated them all and one by one their bodies arrived back at the camp. When Maeve asked more warriors to go out and do single combat they shook their heads and refused.

Cuchulainn waited impatiently at the ford. Then when no other foe appeared he hammered on his shield and shouted, 'Send someone out to me!'

'Will you fight Cuchulainn?' Maeve asked Fergus.

'I can't fight my own foster-son,' he declared.

But she kept on pleading with him and finally he agreed to go out. Cuchulainn was surprised when he saw Fergus approaching the ford. He was even more surprised when he saw that he carried no sword in his scabbard.

'You must be under strong protection,' Cuchulainn said, 'to come against me with no sword.'

'I wouldn't use it on you even if I had one,' Fergus said softly. 'I want you to give way to me.'

Cuchulainn stared at him with a look of puzzlement. 'Why should I do that?' he asked.

'Because of the fostering and friendship I have given you,' Fergus replied. 'Give way to me now.'

Cuchulainn hesitated. He had never yielded to any warrior before. But he was very fond of his foster-father and had no wish to hurt him. 'I'll give way to you,' he said, 'if you promise to yield to me the next time we meet.'

'I promise,' Fergus said.

Cuchulainn turned, went back across the ford, and raced into the hills. A cheer rang out from the camp when Maeve and her men saw Cuchulainn running away.

'Follow him!' Maeve shouted to Fergus.

'I will not,' Fergus called out, walking back to the camp. 'He's gone too far and I'd never catch up with him.'

'Look!' Maeve pointed at the ford. 'The way is clear. Now is our chance!' she urged her warriors. A group of men ran down to the river. Just as they reached it Cuchulainn appeared on a nearby hilltop and sped back to stop them. After a brief battle they all lay dead at his feet. He stood triumphantly in the middle of the ford and challenged more warriors to come out against him.

But none of Maeve's men would accept the challenge. The queen tongue-lashed them, accusing them of cowardice, but still they refused. With a hiss of disgust she turned and strode into her tent. Fergus followed her.

'What will you do now?' he asked.

'I will ask Ferdia to come and fight Cuchulainn,' Maeve replied. 'They are foster brothers. They have trained together and are said to be equal in everything.'

'Except for the Ga Bolga,' Fergus said.

'Ferdia can avoid that,' Maeve declared.

'How?'

'He is covered in battle by a skin of horn that no weapon can pierce.'

Fergus shook his head sadly. A sudden fear seized him that Cuchulainn was about to meet his match at last.

CHAPTER TWELVE

The Fight between the Foster-brothers

FERDIA STARED SUSPICIOUSLY AT THE MESSENGER. He had a fair idea of why Maeve had invited him to her camp. And he had no desire to go and fight his friend and foster-brother Cuchulainn.

'Tell the queen I regret I cannot come,' he said.

The messenger looked at him shrewdly. 'She will think you are afraid,' he observed.

'I am afraid of no one!' Ferdia exclaimed angrily.

'For the sake of your honour then you had better go,' the messenger said.

'Very well,' Ferdia said quietly. 'I will meet the queen and hear what she has to say.'

So he set off with the messenger for Maeve's camp. The queen gave him a great welcome when he arrived. She took him into her tent and ordered her servants to bring food and wine. When he had his fill of everything she smiled and said, 'Well now, do you know why I have asked you here?'

'I don't, ' Ferdia responded. 'But since the noblest men in Ireland are here why shouldn't I be here too?'

'Why not indeed,' the queen said softly. 'Are you not the greatest warrior in the land?' She paused and added, 'That is why I sent for you. I want you to do battle with Cuchulainn.'

'No, that's impossible,' Ferdia began to say, but Maeve raised her hand to cut him short.

'Wait,' she said, 'until you hear what I am offering you. I will give you half my treasure, and my own daughter in marriage, and my everlasting friendship on top of it all.'

Ferdia slowly shook his head. 'Those are great rewards,' he said. 'But great as they are I would sooner leave them with you than go out and fight my own foster-brother.'

There was a brief silence. Then Maeve sighed and said, 'What Cuchulainn said must be true so.'

'What did he say?' Ferdia asked.

'He boasted that he could defeat you in combat.'

'He did?' Ferdia's face reddened with anger. He thumped his fist on the table. 'In that case I'll be the first man to fight him tomorrow!'

Maeve smiled grimly. 'And then he shall surely die,' she whispered.

Fergus had been listening outside the queen's tent. He decided to go to Cuchulainn and tell him what Maeve had arranged.

Cuchulainn was surprised to see him arriving at the ford. 'What brings you here?' he asked.

'You should know who's coming to fight you tomorrow morning,' Fergus said.

'Who?'

'Your own foster-brother, Ferdia.'

'I don't want to fight him,' Cuchulainn said. 'Not because I fear him but because I love him.'

'Perhaps you should fear him too,' Fergus said. 'When he fights he wears a skin of horn that no weapon can pierce.'

Cuchulainn shrugged. 'We shall see what happens tomorrow,' he said. And he crossed back over the ford and lay down to rest.

Early next morning Ferdia went out to fight Cuchulainn. They met in the middle of the ford.

'You are welcome,' Ferdia said.

'I could trust your welcome once', Cuchulainn said sadly, 'but I don't trust it now. You did wrong to come to fight me.'

'I can't go back now,' Ferdia said. 'If I refuse to fight you I'll be shamed forever.'

'Let us begin then,' Cuchulainn said. 'Since you reached the ford first you have the choice of weapons until nightfall.'

'We'll fight with spears and shields,' Ferdia decided.

Cuchulainn nodded and the combat commenced.

Shield clattered against shield with a deafening noise that sent flocks of birds scattering through the air. Spear rattled against spear in a mist of flying sparks. They fought like that all day and when nightfall came neither of them had gained any advantage over the other.

'It's time to break off,' Ferdia said.

'Very well,' Cuchulainn agreed, and crossing back over the river he lay down on the bank to rest. Ferdia returned to Maeve's camp.

Next morning they met again in the middle of the ford. 'You have the choice of weapons today,' Ferdia said.

'We'll fight with horse and chariot,' Cuchulainn said.

They leaped into their chariots, raised their long stabbing spears, and whipped up their horses into a wild gallop. The chariots passed so close to one another that a feather could not have fitted between the wheels. Their spears collided and bent, twanging like bow-strings after each clash. When the sun at last began to set, their horses were ready to drop with exhaustion.

'Let us break off now,' Cuchulainn called out, 'for our horses are tired and so are we.'

They climbed down stiffly from their chariots and went away to rest for the night.

Early on the third day they came to meet each other in the middle of the ford. 'What is your choice of weapons?' Cuchulainn asked.

'Broad swords and long shields,' Ferdia replied. 'This time we'll fight in the river.'

They got their weapons ready and stood in the ford water confronting each other.

'This may be our final struggle,' Ferdia said.

Cuchulainn nodded and the fight began. The huge swords cleaved through the air and battered on the knobs of their shields. They hacked and hewed until their shields were split from top to bottom. The rasp of the sword-blades echoed over the plain as they collided. But neither of the warriors could gain advantage over the other. So fiercely did they fight that the river was driven from its course with the trampling of their feet, leaving a dry space in the ford.

Then Ferdia saw a hole in Cuchulainn's shield and made a sudden lunge through it with his sword. It pierced Cuchulainn's chest and blood gushed from the wound. Cuchulainn reeled back. Ferdia followed him, wounding him again.

'Send the Ga Bolga down to me on the stream,' Cuchulainn called out to Laeg. But the charioteer saw that the ford was dry and that the weapon would not reach him. So he hastily built a dam, sending the river back on course. Then he sent the Ga Bolga gliding down. Cuchulainn caught it with his toe and drove it through a gap in Ferdia's skin of horn. Every part of his body was filled with deadly barbs. Ferdia fell dead in the middle of the ford.

Cuchulainn picked him up and carried him back across the river. He laid him down gently and then lay down himself for he was weak from his wounds. He stared sadly at the body of his foster-brother.

'You should have listened to me, Ferdia,' he whispered. 'Then you would still be alive.'

His eyes closed suddenly. Laeg ran to him thinking he was dead.

CHAPTER THIRTEEN

Maeve Is Defeated

A LOOK OF RELIEF CAME OVER LAEG'S FACE when he found that Cuchulainn was still breathing. He set to work at once, cleaning Cuchulainn's wounds and covering them with healing herbs. He shook his head with dismay. He knew it would take days for Cuchulainn to recover.

But who would defend the province in the meantime? King Conor and his warriors still lay in enchanted sleep at Eman Macha. Nothing now stood in Maeve's way. As soon as she realised that, she would order her army to cross the river. They would come upon the unconscious figure of Cuchulainn and kill him!

Laeg stood up and stared anxiously over at the queen's camp. Everything there was quiet. Maeve and her men were waiting for Cuchulainn to reappear at the ford.

Laeg turned in alarm as he heard the sudden sound of a horse's hooves. Then he smiled as he recognised the tall nobleman who was approaching. It was Cuchulainn's father, Sualdam.

'I was on my way to Eman Macha when I heard that Cuchulainn was here,' Sualdam said. He paused and stared down at his son lying unconscious on the ground. 'What has happened to leave him in this sorry state?'

Laeg explained about Cuchulainn's stand against the warriors of Maeve. 'It will be some time before he regains his strength. And in the meantime there is nobody to defend Ulster.'

'Where are Conor and his men?' Sualdam asked.

'A magic spell has been placed on them,' Laeg said. 'They are all sound asleep in the palace.'

'I shall go there now and try and awaken them!' Sualdam said quickly. He wheeled his horse around and galloped away.

Laeg turned and with a worried expression watched the enemy's camp again. His heart gave a skip as a warrior emerged carrying his weapons. The man came down halfway to the river and stared in puzzlement at the unguarded ford. Then he turned slowly and walked back to the camp. Laeg shook his head. It would not be long until Maeve understood that nobody now was in her way. He had better put Cuchulainn into the chariot and take him off to a place of safety. Maeve's men would kill him if he left him where he was. He hurried back to where Cuchulainn was lying.

Cuchulainn's eyes flickered open and he stared up at Laeg. 'Your father was here,' Laeg said. 'He has gone to Eman Macha to see if he can arouse King Conor and his men.'

'That will take time,' Cuchulainn whispered. He raised himself up on his elbow. 'I must guard the ford!'

'But you are too weak to fight,' Laeg protested.

Cuchulainn nodded. 'I know that', he said, 'but my enemies don't.' Grimacing with pain he rose to his feet. 'Help me down to the water's edge while it is dark. Tie me to a boulder there and put my sword in my hand. Then leave me there alone. When my enemies see me in the morning they will think I have recovered.'

So Laeg brought Cuchulainn down to the river and tied him securely to the boulder. He placed a sword in Cuchulainn's hand and reluctantly went away. When Maeve and her men looked out next morning they saw with dismay that Cuchulainn had returned.

Sualdam meanwhile had arrived at Eman Macha. He rode up to the palace gates and shouted, 'Wake up, men of Ulster! Come and defend your province against Maeve and her warriors.'

There was no response from inside the palace. Sualdam shouted again but still there was no answer. He tried to open the gates but they were locked. He shook his head impatiently and circled the palace walls looking for a place low enough for his horse to jump over.

His eyes lit up when he saw a suitable place. He set the horse in a gallop towards it and the animal sailed up and over into the palace grounds.

As they landed, the shield on Sualdam's back broke loose from its strap. It flew over his shoulder and the sharp rim sliced through his neck. His head spun through the air and rolled along the ground until it came to rest under a palace window.

'Wake up, men of Ulster!' the head called out. 'Come and defend your province against Maeve and her warriors!'

The power of the spell on the men inside was already beginning to fade. The warning shout through the window now jerked them into wakefulness. They rubbed their eyes and listened in astonishment as the voice continued to call out.

King Conor jumped up and crashed his fist on the table. 'Get ready for battle!' he ordered. His men scrambled to their feet, grabbed their weapons, and raced to their horses.

Back at the ford the grim figure of Cuchulainn still kept Maeve's army at bay. But his head was beginning to sag and a glazed look came into his eyes. Only the thongs that tied him to the boulder prevented him from slumping to the ground.

Maeve was watching him from her camp. After a while she suspected that something was wrong. 'Cuchulainn hasn't moved from that rock all day,' she said to Fergus. 'Perhaps he is weaker than we think.'

'It may be just a trick to lure your men out,' Fergus cautioned.

'But look at the way his head droops,' Maeve said, 'He seems too weak to fight.' She laughed suddenly and said, 'There's only one way to find out.'

She called one of her warriors and asked him to go to the ford. The man hesitated and was about to shake his head when Maeve said, 'I don't want you to do combat with Cuchulainn. If he moves to attack you come back here.'

The warrior walked down to the river. He stared nervously at Cuchulainn, ready for flight at the first sign of danger. But Cuchulainn did not move. After a while the warrior grew bolder. He picked up a stone and threw it at Cuchulainn. Then he began to jeer him. There was still no move from Cuchulainn. The warrior turned and called out, 'The demon is powerless!'

A loud cheer came from the camp. 'Come on!' Maeve shouted. 'There is nothing now to stop us!'

She leaped into her chariot and drove quickly to the ford. Her men followed her, waving their swords and spears. Laeg watched in despair as the triumphant army surged towards the river. Cuchulainn would soon be dead. Laeg seized his weapons. He would die fighting beside him! Then, just as he was about to run down to the ford, he heard the thunder of hooves behind him and the harsh shouts of angry men. He looked around and jumped with joy. The warriors of Ulster had arrived to do battle!

The two armies clashed in the river. Swords slashed and spears jabbed, turning the water into a churning stream of blood. For a

whole day the battle raged fiercely. Then Maeve's warriors began to give way. Sensing victory, King Conor gave a great shout of triumph. But it died away on his lips when he saw his old enemy Fergus rallying the retreating men and leading them in a savage attack that pushed the Ulstermen back over the river. They were cut down like ripe wheat as Fergus swept through them with his great two-handled sword.

A sudden battle-spasm came over Cuchulainn. He broke the thongs that held him to the boulder and rushed into the fight. His sword carved a path through the men opposing him and then suddenly he came face-to-face with Fergus.

For a moment they stared at each other. Then Cuchulainn said, 'Remember your promise. Give way to me.'

'Very well,' Fergus said, and he withdrew from the battle, followed by his men.

When Maeve and her warriors saw this they turned and fled. Cuchulainn raced after her and caught up with her. The queen's eyes opened wide with fear. 'Spare me,' she pleaded.

Cuchulainn slowly lowered his sword. 'You deserve to be killed,' he said. 'But I will spare you, provided you promise never to invade Ulster again.'

'I promise,' she said.

Cuchulainn let her go then and she hurried back to her palace at Cruachan. 'At least I still have the Brown Bull of Cooley,' she consoled herself as she arrived at the gates.

But soon she was to lose that also.

CHAPTER FOURTEEN

The Brown Bull Escapes

MAEVE STRODE INTO THE FIELD where her husband Ailill was admiring his bull Finnbeannach. 'I've a much finer animal than that,' she said.

Ailill laughed scornfully. 'You'd nothing to equal Finnbeannach when we compared our herds,' he reminded her.

'Well, I do now!' she snapped and calling her servants she ordered them to bring the Brown Bull of Cooley to the field.

Ailill's face fell when he saw the magnificent animal. 'You see?' Maeve crowed. 'I am richer than you after all.'

But she had hardly finished speaking when the Brown Bull bellowed angrily and suddenly attacked Finnbeannach. After a short fierce fight, Ailill's bull lay dead on the ground. Ailill drew his sword. 'I will kill that animal of yours!' he shouted.

Maeve tried to hold him back but he broke free from her grip and advanced on the Brown Bull. As Maeve ran after Ailill, the bull bellowed again and made a sudden charge at them. They stopped, turned, and ran for their lives. They raced into the palace and closed the massive door behind them. The bull's horns thudded into the door. Then he shook his head and scattering everybody before him escaped into the hills. Maeve sent her herdsmen out to look for him but they never found him again.

Daire Mac Fiachna was sitting in his house in Cooley when he heard a familiar bellow outside. He could hardly believe his ears. He rushed to the window and looked out. The Brown Bull had come home! His face glowed with joy as he hurried out to welcome his treasure.

And so the *Táin* ended.

CHILDREN'S BOOKS
FROM THE O'BRIEN PRESS

Send for our catalogue.
Order books from your bookseller - or in case of difficulty from
The O'Brien Press, 20 Victoria Road, Dublin 6, Ireland.

BIKE HUNT

A Story of Thieves and Kidnappers
Hugh Galt
An exciting story, set in Dublin
and county Wicklow - winner of
the Young People's Books medal
in the Irish Book Awards. PB£3.95

CYRIL

The Tale of an Orphaned Squirrel
*Eugene McCabe - illustrated by Al O'-
Donnell*
A moving story set in nature - win-
ner of the Reading Association
Award. PB £3.95

JIMEEN

A Comic Irish Classic
*Pádraig O Siochfhradha - illustrated
by Brian Bourke*
The first English translation of the
much-loved antics of this madcap
character. PB £3.50

THE LUCKY BAG

Classic Irish Children's Stories
*Ed. Eilis Dillon, Pat Donlon, Pat
Egan and Peter Fallon
- illustrated by Martin Gale*
A collection of the best in Irish
children's literature. PB £4.95

THE LOST ISLAND

*Eilis Dillon - illustrated by David
Rooney*
The mystery and danger of the sea
in this gripping adventure story.
PB £3.95

FAERY NIGHTS/
OICHEANTA SÍ

Micheál Mac Liammóir
A unique treasury of Celtic stories
in dual language texts and illustrated by the author. PB £3.50

THE LITTLE BLACK
SHEEP

*Written and illustrated by Elizabeth
Shaw*
A simple, charming book to
delight the younger child. Boards
£3.95

ZANY TALES

*Pat Ingoldsby - illustrated by Frances
Hyland*
A collection of hilarious off-the-
wall tales for younger children.
PB £3.95

HEROIC TALES from the Ulster Cycle
Classic stories derived from ancient Irish Legends. PB £3.50

THE COOL MAC COOL
Gordon Snell - Illustrated by Wendy Shea
The life and times of legendary Celtic hero Finn MacCool. PB £4.95

EXPLORING THE BOOK OF KELLS
George Otto Simms
Illustrated by David Rooney & Eoin O'Brien
A world-renowned authority offers a compact guide to an outstanding national treasure. HB £6.95

BRENDAN THE NAVIGATOR
Explorer of the Ancient World
George Otto Simms
Illustrated by David Rooney
One of the great adventures of the world. Made famous by Tim Severin. HB £6.95

JANEY MACK ME SHIRT IS BLACK
Eamonn MacThomáis
The street rhymes, stories and incidents of bygone Dublin PB £4.50

TOMMY -THE THEATRE CAT
Maureen Potter - illustrated by David Rooney
A charming tale of backstage theatre life by this well-known entertainer.
PB £3.95

CHRISTMAS WONDER
Craftwork, Lore, Poems, Songs and Stories
Seán C. O'Leary - various illustrations
A lively collection of Irish traditions and lore, with lots of things to make and do. PB £5.95

Busy Fingers - Art and Craft Series
1 Spring
2 Summer
3 Autumn/Halloween
4 Christmas/Winter

Seán C. O'Leary
A popular collection of simple and attractive things to make throughout the year. PB £1.95 each Also available as a pack of four books £7.50

O'Brien Junior Biography Library

The Irish Times praised the books as
'...short, entertaining and full of great pictures.'

1 WOLFE TONE
2 W.B. YEATS
3 GRANUAILE
4 BOB GELDOF

Mary Moriarty and Catherine Sweeney
Major world figures in simple accessible language. Beautifully illustrated.
Watch out for more titles.
PB£3.95 each

DECÓ SERIES

Séamus O-hUltachain and Breandán O Mordha's refreshingly new and popular approach to Irish.
Watch out for the RTE TV Series.

DECÓ 1
Decó agus a Chairde
PB£2.95
DECÓ 2
Craic agus Crofbhriseadh
PB£2.95
DECÓ 3
Saoire an tSamhraidh
PB£2.95

CHILDREN'S TAPES

The Boyne Valley Book and Tape of IRISH LEGENDS
Brenda Maguire - illustrated by Peter Haigh
Favourite legends told by: Gay Byrne, Cyril Cusack, Maureen Potter, Rosaleen Linehan, John B. Keane, Twink. *Book & tape £6.95*

TELL ME A STORY, PAT
Pat Ingoldsby
Eight stories, seven poems - over an hour of fantasy, fun and magic.
£4.95